BROWN COW,
Green Grass,
Yellow
Mellow
Sun

To Kathy Wilson Crook
—E. J.

To my husband, Merlin
—V. R.

Text © 1995 by Ellen Jackson.
Illustrations © 1995 by Victoria Raymond.
All rights reserved.
Printed in Singapore.
For information address Hyperion Books for Children,
114 Fifth Avenue, New York, New York 10011.

FIRST EDITION
1 3 5 7 9 10 8 6 4 2

Jackson, Ellen B.
Brown Cow, Green Grass, Yellow Mellow Sun/Ellen Jackson; illustrated by Victoria Raymond—1st ed.
p. cm.
Summary: A young boy learns about colors in a day at the farm.
ISBN 0-7868-0010-0 (trade)—ISBN 0-7868-2006-3 (lib. bdg.)
[1. Color—Fiction. 2. Farm life—Fiction] I. Raymond, Victoria, ill. II. Title. PZ7. J13247Br 1995
[E]—dc20 93-37091 CIP AC

Each illustration for this book is constructed from many separate elements,
each of which is first sculpted from a colored modeling compound
called Sculpey III and then baked in an oven until hard.
Once each component of the piece is complete,
the artist paints them with acrylic paints and then—using glue,
armature wire, and even toothpicks—assembles the pieces into what the reader sees.

This book is set in 36-point Times Roman and multiple point sizes of
Ponderosa, Birch, Party, Lambada, and Bernhard Antigua Bold Condensed.

Photography by Monica Stevenson.

Design by Karen Palinko.

BROWN COW, Green Grass, Yellow Mellow Sun

ELLEN JACKSON

BROWN COW,
Green Grass,
Yellow Mellow Sun

ILLUSTRATED BY
VICTORIA RAYMOND

Hyperion Books for Children
NEW YORK

A
yellow sun
gleamed
in the
blue sky.

The
Yellow mellow sunlight
warmed the earth.

The grass grew
green and tall.

Along walked a
BROWN COW.

MUNCH

MUNCH MUNCH

MUNCH

The **COW** ate the green grass.

MUNCH. MUNCH.

The **BROWN COW** grew

bigger and BIGGER.

Along walked a **boy**.

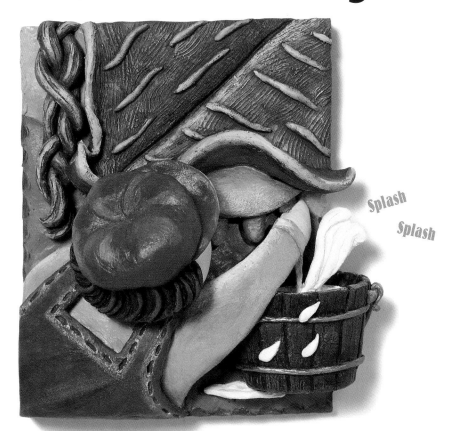

Splash
Splash

"From that **BIG BROWN COW**
I will get **white milk**," he said.
Splash! Splash!

The **boy** gave the

white milk

to his *granny.*

"I will make

something good,"

said *Granny.*

She put the
white, bright milk
in a churn.

Churn

Churn
Churn

Churn. Churn.

Granny sang softly:

"From the yellow

mellow sun
came the
green, green grass.

"From the
green, green grass
came the

BIG
BROWN
COW.

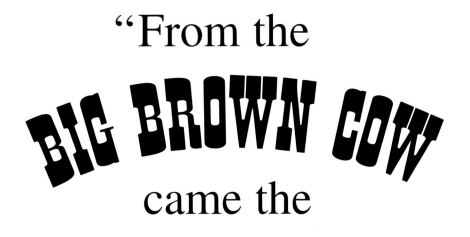

"From the **BIG BROWN COW** came the

white, bright milk.

"From the **white,**

bright milk came . . . ."

Granny stopped singing. She opened up the churn and scraped the bottom with a long wooden spoon.

"BUTTER~

yellow mellow butter," sang Granny.

BIG BROWN PANCAKES

To make pancakes you will need:

1 cup all-purpose flour
1 tablespoon sugar
2 teaspoons baking powder
1/4 teaspoon salt
1 egg
1 cup milk
2 tablespoons cooking oil

First, stir together the flour, sugar, baking powder, and salt in a bowl. Set aside. In a separate bowl, beat the egg until fluffy. Add the milk and oil to the egg. Stir together. Add to the dry ingredients all at once. Stir until slightly lumpy. For each pancake, pour a few tablespoons of batter onto a hot, lightly greased griddle. Turn the pancake over when its surface is bubbly and looks slightly dry around the edges. This recipe makes eight to ten Big Brown Pancakes.

YELLOW MELLOW BUTTER

To make homemade butter to go with your homemade pancakes, pour one pint of room-temperature whipping cream into a jar or other container with a secure lid. With lid in place, shake the jar for 20 to 30 minutes and . . . BUTTER! Yellow Mellow Butter.